Cruz Coyote & Rory Roadrunner

By Yasmin John-Thorpe Illustrated by Endrené Shepherd

This book is dedicated to all those young readers who love animals and believe they can talk to each other. I wrote this book because of my interest in the relationships between Sonoran Desert animals.

Thanks to the website of the Governor of Arizona, where my research took me for information:
azgovernor.gov/AZSpotlight/Kids_Wildlife.asp

Thank you to the families, who read the first draft of the story and offered insight:
Traci Santos and her children, Lance and Blake Lewis
Greg and Vicki Rodgers and their children, Andrew and Zachary.

My sincere appreciation to:
Illustrator - Endrené Shepherd; Editor/Proofreader - Norma Hill; Typesetter - Dawn Renaud

Back cover photos:
Yasmin, Stuart Bish Photography; Endrené, Bryce B K Beckett

John-Thorpe, Yasmin, 1950-, author
Cruz Coyote & Rory Roadrunner / by Yasmin John-Thorpe; illustrated by Endrené Shepherd.
ISBN 978-1540382979 (pbk. in US)
ISBN 978-0-9921245-4-0 (pbk. in Canada)
I. Shepherd, Endrené, 1979-, illustrator II. Title. III. Title:
Cruz Coyote and Rory Roadrunner.

PS8619.O446C78 2014 jC813'.6 C2014-907387-9

Books in this series:

For babies

What Am I?

Goodnight, Sonoran Friends

For readers to 8 years

A Home for the Q's

Cruz Coyote & Rory Roadrunner

The Adventures of Cruz Coyote

Cruz and the Pack

The Adventures of Hummer Hummingbird

Jenry, the Silly Javelina

A Tale of Horned Owls

Other books, for readers 8 to 14 years:

Grandpa's Gift - recounting the Canadians' WWI Battle to win Vimy Ridge

Two Unlikely Heroes of the New World - an adventure story of a young Spaniard and his Mayan friend

Just Nuts - a book about various kinds of nuts and nut allergies

All of Yasmin John-Thorpe's books are available on amazon.com under the author's name.

About the Characters

Cruz Coyote - Cruz is a **desert coyote**. This is a smaller coyote with a lighter-tinted coat. They are naturally curious animals who roam the hot desert and hunt small rodents and insects. Unlike most coyotes, who live in packs with other coyotes, Cruz lives and hunts alone.

Rory Roadrunner - Rory is a **roadrunner**—a bird and a member of the **cuckoo** family. Roadrunners prefer walking or running and can reach speeds of seventeen miles per hour. If they sense danger or are traveling downhill, they can fly. Their large bodies can stay airborne for only a few seconds.

Hummer Hummingbird - Hummer is an **Anna's hummingbird.** This species has been named after Anna Masséna, Duchess of Rivoli. The male bird has vibrant coloring. A hummingbird's long beak reaches deep into flowers to gather nectar. During courtship the male climbs to 130 feet in the air, then dives toward the female with a burst of noises produced by air passing through its tail feathers.

Suzy Spider - Suzy is a **black widow spider**. The female black widow is the most venomous spider in America. It is shiny and black with a red hourglass mark on its belly. It hangs upside down so you can easily see this marking.

Toby Toad - Toby is a **Sonoran desert toad.** One of the largest toads in North America, it has olive-green and brown skin. It mostly lives underground, but surfaces during the monsoon season. The female can lay up to eight thousand eggs. This toad will eat almost any living thing it can fit in its mouth. The toxins on its skin can kill a dog.

Gavin Gecko - Gavin is a **gecko**, which is a type of lizard. Most cannot blink because they have no eyelids. The gecko's specialized toe pads allow it to easily climb smooth and vertical surfaces. It eats insects.

Quinn and Queenie Quail - Quinn and Queenie are **Gambel's quails** - a species named after William Gambel, a naturalist, who saw the birds in 1841 while collecting animals and plants for the Academy of Natural Sciences of Philadelphia. Large groups of quails live in a covey. Gambel's quails are russet-colored, while **California quails** are blue and gray. Females lay about ten to twelve eggs. They sit on these eggs until the chicks hatch, which takes from twenty-one to twenty-three days.

Tish Tortoise - Tish is a **desert tortoise**. This is the only tortoise to live under the extreme conditions of the desert, where ground temperatures exceed 140 degrees Fahrenheit. The desert tortoise digs underground burrows to escape the heat of summer and cold of winter, spending 95 percent of its time underground. It digs holes to collect rain water after monsoons, and eats herbs, grasses, some shrubs and new growth cacti and their flowers. A desert tortoise can live to be between fifty and eighty years old.

Sammie Squirrel - Sammie is a **round-tailed ground squirrel**. It is called a ground squirrel because it burrows in loose soil under creosote bushes and mesquite trees. This squirrel is sandy-colored, matching the soil it burrows into. It eats green vegetation, seeds, ants, termites and grasshoppers. In winter, it lives underground.

After an adventurous night of hunting in the Sonoran Desert of southwestern Arizona, Cruz Coyote is tired. Unlike other coyotes, he does not belong to a pack. He lives and hunts alone. As the sun climbs in the morning sky, Cruz settles down near some tall grasses.

"That was hard work," Cruz says, yawning. "Now I need sleep."

Through slowly closing eyes, Cruz notices two quails close by under a skeleton saguaro. Cruz looks around. "Are these quails alone, with no family, like me?"

Whizz! Cruz feels something buzz by his head. A hummingbird hovers above. "What–?"

"You are a *bad* coyote," the bird yells. "Leave the quails alone!" With another *whizz*, it zooms away.

"What a silly bird," Cruz says, checking on the two quails. He sees them disappearing from view. Even though he needs to get some sleep, Cruz rises and stretches, before crouching behind the bushes.

"Let me see what these quails are up to," Cruz chuckles as he follows them.

Not far away, Rory Roadrunner wakes to the bright sunshine of the Sonoran Desert. Rory loves to run fast and is proud he can fly away if a large snake, a coyote or a bobcat chases after him.

"I must find breakfast," Rory says. Hopping down from his perch in a mesquite tree, he goes in search of something to eat, keeping a lookout for Razor Rattlesnake, Cruz Coyote and Bryce Bobcat.

Rory captures a small rodent trying to scurry away. He is still hungry, so he hunts for other morsels. He spies a black widow spider spinning her web.

"You are too close to the edge of that branch, Suzy Spider," Rory squeaks up to her. "If I try to get you I will fall. But I might grab *you*, Gavin Gecko," he says to the gecko watching the spider. Before Rory can grab him, though, Gavin Gecko quickly wiggles away.

Rory hops up to a branch of a nearby tree to check for nests with eggs. He notices a pair of quails gathering sticks and dry leaves before disappearing under dense bushes.

"Aha!" says Rory. "Someone is building a nest." He hops down to find a safe place to spy on the quails without being seen. Rory knows it takes days for a quail to lay eggs and for the chicks to hatch. He is patient. Soon, he will be able to steal tasty quail eggs, and maybe quail chicks.

Cruz Coyote continues to follow the quails. He watches as they go under dense arroyo bushes. He waits, but they do not come out.

"Are they going to make their home here?" he wonders. Cruz wishes he could ask the quails what they are up to. He finds a place above the quails' hideout where he can keep watch. Finally, waiting for the quails to come out again, Cruz falls asleep.

Boom! Rory Roadrunner is spying on the quails when the loud noise startles him.

"What is happening?" he yells. He sees dark clouds overhead and he hears low thunder. These send him racing for cover. A nasty monsoon storm bursts overhead.

"Whoa!" cries Rory, as large drops of rain pelt him. Quickly, he seeks refuge under a cluster of large yucca plants.

Cruz Coyote watches the roadrunner's mad dash. Cruz hurries to find cover under a mesquite tree.

As the storm rages, the water rushing across the parched landscape uncovers a large toad. When the rain stops, Cruz shakes off his wet fur and approaches the toad.

"Don't get close to Toby Toad!" yells the hummingbird sitting on a nearby saguaro. "His skin is covered with poison. If you lick him you will die. Don't you know anything?"

Cruz moves off without answering. He does not know about toads or quails. He has no one to teach him about life in the desert. He is alone, without family and friends.

“Better see how the quails are doing,” Rory Roadrunner says, as the storm passes. After he shakes himself to get rid of the rain clinging to his feathers, Rory moves back to his original position to check on the quails.

“Looks like the nest is ready,” whispers Rory. “Soon there will be eggs in there.”

Rory does not know that Cruz is watching both him and the quails.

Cruz Coyote sees the comings and goings of the quails. "What can they be doing?" he wonders.

Unlike Rory, Cruz has no idea what the quails are up to. He moves this way and that trying to see under the brushy area.

Then, unable to stop the hunger gnawing at his stomach, Cruz checks on Rory before heading off to find food.

On the opposite side of the wash, Rory Roadrunner still has no idea Cruz is close by, keeping watch on his comings and goings.

Rory smacks his lips. "Yummy," he chuckles. He leaves the quails to build their home, lay eggs and hatch babies. After making a note of where to return to find the quails, Rory hurries off in search of something to eat.

The next morning, Cruz crouches low as the male quail hurries off from under the bushy arroyo. Cruz is so close that he sees the female quail hiding at the edge of the bushes.

Soon a desert tortoise approaches the area close to where the quail is standing.

"Hello," Cruz hears the quail call. Then she asks, "Where are you off to?"

"Who are you and why do you ask?" drones the tortoise.

"Forgive my rudeness," the quail says. "I'm Queenie Quail, and my mate is Quinn."

"Good morning. I'm Tish Tortoise," replies Tish. "I'm off to get water."

"You are? Where?" asks the quail.

"Ha," chuckles Tish. "I dig holes to gather water when it rains. It rained not long ago. My watering holes now hold a drink for me. See you," Tish calls, slowly moving on.

Days pass as Cruz Coyote still wonders what the quails are doing under the bushes. He notices only the male quail, Quinn, going in and out.

"What has happened to Queenie, the female quail?" Cruz wonders. Then, he remembers he has not seen Rory for several days. "Has Rory been here while I am busy finding my own dinner?"

After waiting a few more days, Cruz creeps closer to the bushes where the quails are. His brownish fur helps him blend in with the dirt and dry grasses. Suddenly a baby desert ground squirrel rushes out of a hole on the other side of the quails' cover. She disappears under the area where the quails are staying.

Staying low, Cruz listens.

"Whatcha doing?" Cruz hears the squirrel asks Queenie.
"I'm keeping my eggs warm," Queenie answers.
"What are eggs?"
"They hold my baby chicks inside," says Queenie.
"Why?" asks the squirrel.
"It is how I have children."
"Can I peek?" asks the squirrel. "Wow! How many are there?"
"Eleven," answers Queenie.
"How long will you sit on them?"
"I have been sitting on them for many days. I have to keep them warm as they will hatch soon," Queenie explains. "You do have a lot of questions. What's your name?"
"Sammie Squirrel. What's your name?"
"I'm Queenie Quail, and that is Quinn, over there."

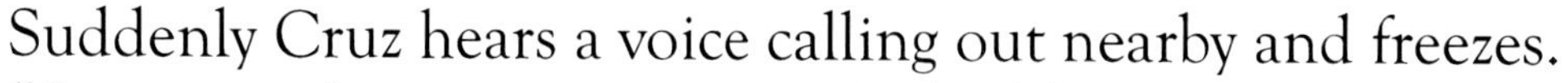

Suddenly Cruz hears a voice calling out nearby and freezes.

"Sammie, where are you? Time for bed!" A mother ground squirrel pokes her head out of the same hole her daughter had come from earlier.

"Coming!" yells Sammie. "Bye!" She rushes to the hole that leads to her home. "Mom, there is a quail sitting on eggs to get babies and ... "

The rest of what Sammie says is lost as she disappears down into the hole.

Cruz stays still for a long time. Finally, he peeks into the thick bushes. He sees one quail sitting on dry grasses and sticks. Her back is to him. As he watches, she shifts her body and Cruz glimpses small, round spotted things under her. *What did she call them? Oh, yes. Eggs.* As quietly as he can, Cruz moves back to his lookout spot.

"Those must be eggs, okay! But, babies? What are those?" Cruz mumbles, before he falls asleep.

The cries from the quails wake Cruz. He sees Quinn and Queenie Quail emerge with little quails. *These must be babies*, Cruz thinks. They are tiny versions of the parents. They scurry this way and that, following the adult male and female.

Out of nowhere, Rory Roadrunner rushes in and grabs two quail chicks. Cruz hears Queenie's warning call. It scatters the others back to safety, and Queenie takes off after Rory Roadrunner.

"Stop," Queenie cries. "Please, stop!"

Cruz runs forward, blocking the roadrunner's mad dash, and Rory comes to a halt.

Quinn and Queenie catch up and try to peck at him to make him drop their babies. "Drop them!" they scream.

Cruz Coyote's paw slams Rory Roadrunner to the ground.

"Drop them," he demands.

Rory Roadrunner opens his beak and drops the chicks.

Queenie rushes to them.

Cruz sees both are alive, although one limps and the other holds one wing at an odd angle.

Cruz Coyote stares at the quails. His paw remains on Rory Roadrunner's chest.

"So those are babies?" Cruz asks.

"You cannot take them," Queenie yells.

Cruz looks at the adult quails. "You are Quinn and Queenie, right?" he asks.

Quinn and Queenie seem surprised. "Yes," Quinn answers.

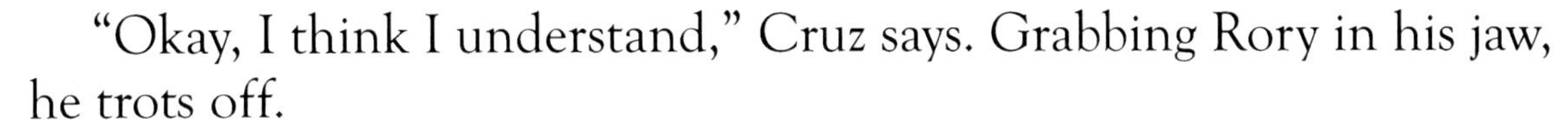

"Okay, I think I understand," Cruz says. Grabbing Rory in his jaw, he trots off.

"What just happened?" Cruz hears Quinn ask.

"I don't know," Queenie answers. "I don't understand any of it. That coyote saved our babies. I am happy he did not turn on them or us. Let's gather our chicks and take them home."

Cruz turns to see the quails shoo their family back to the safety of their home, and then he keeps moving farther away with Rory Roadrunner as his prize.

The End

Cruz Coyote & Rory Roadrunner

COMPREHENSION EXERCISE

Readers, test your knowledge:

1. Where does Cruz Coyote live?
2. When can Rory Roadrunner fly? What kind of bird is he?
3. What did Quinn and Queenie Quail build under the bushes?
4. Who warns Cruz Coyote not to lick Toby Toad? Why?
5. Do you remember why Tish Tortoise has water to drink?
6. What was Rory Roadrunner waiting for?
7. What does Sammie Squirrel want to know?
8. How many quail's eggs are there?
9. Who is a hero after he saves the baby quails?

ISBN 978-1540382702 (U.S.A.)
ISBN 978-0-9921245-2-6 (Canada)

Quinn and Queenie are quails on the move. They have left their old covey, seeking to find a new home before the monsoon rains arrive.

Their search takes them across the Sonoran Desert, where they meet new friends and avoid dangerous predators.

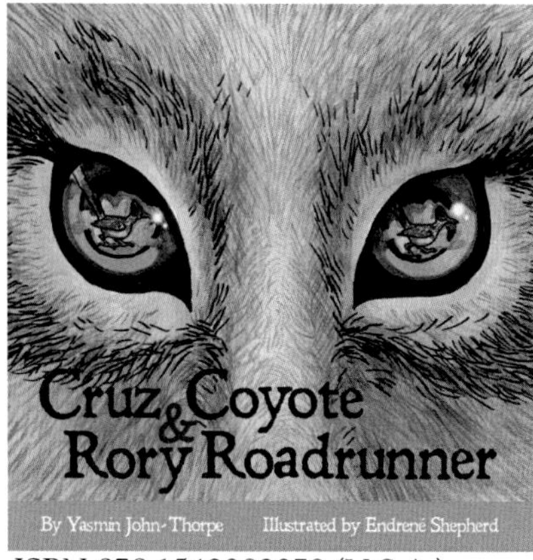

ISBN 978-1540382979 (U.S.A.)
ISBN 978-0-9921245-4-0 (Canada)

Cruz Coyote lives alone in the Sonoran Desert. Curious about the different creatures he meets, he watches two quails make a hiding place in some bushes. What are they up to?

Rory Roadrunner watches the birds too. He knows what they are doing, and he is waiting hungrily.

What will Cruz and Rory do when those quail eggs hatch?

ISBN 978-1518795855 (U.S.A.)
ISBN 978-0-9921245-6-4 (Canada)

Cruz Coyote is growing up alone in the Sonoran Desert.

How is he to learn about all the other desert animals?

ISBN: 978-1537462042 (U.S.A.)
ISBN: 978-0-9921245-7-1 (Canada)

Cruz Coyote has made friends with Charlie, a young pup. The leader of Charlie's pack says Cruz can join them, but first he must do something for the pack.

Will Cruz do it?

ISBN: 978-1977535771 (U.S.A.)
ISBN: 978-0-9959843-1-8 (Canada)

Hummer Hummingbird is injured, so he must leave his friend Cruz Coyote and the pack behind to search for a safe place to heal. His journey across the Sonoran Desert to a hideaway nest is full of danger. Hummer must stay alert as he dodges predator birds wishing to take him to their families as dinner. Follow Hummer's flight to safety as he encounters friends and foes along his path.

ISBN: 978-1726493581 (U.S.A.)

Jenry, the "spare" javelina, has a problem. Why does he have to follow his family and dine on prickly pear cacti every evening? Jenry runs off from family and safety, in search of a rodent or small animal he can capture and eat.

What awaits Jenry? Will he be successful? Which friends or predators will he encounter on his wild adventure? Will he be safe without his family's protection?

ISBN: 978-1976577956 (U.S.A.)
ISBN: 978-0-9959843-2-5 (Canada)

Goodnight, Sonoran Friends introduces some of the desert creatures in the Sonoran Desert series.

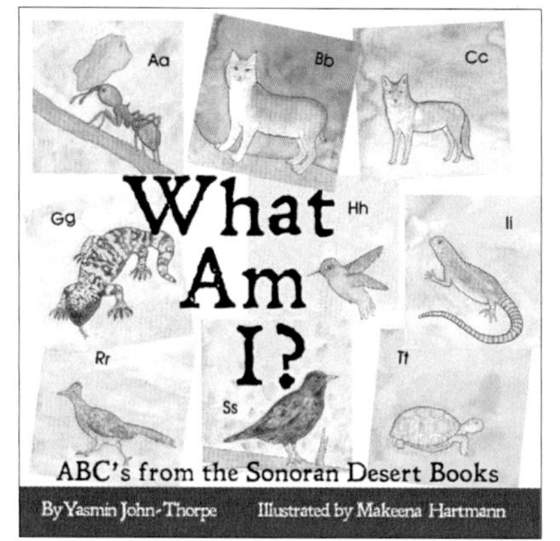

ISBN: 9781692812843 (U.S.A.)

What Am I? ABC's from the Sonoran Desert Books Meet some of the animals, birds, and plants of the Sonoran Desert. This book for early readers features familiar characters from this series, and introduces new ones, too, along with a few desert features. The entire alphabet is represented, from *a*nt to *z*ebra-tail lizard and all the letters in between!

ISBN: 9781080787852 (U.S.A.)

Odin and Ossana Owl are raising four young owlets in a small nest perched precariously in a palm tree. The human residents of Quail Creek watch anxiously as little Odette falls from the nest, followed a few days later by Oakie. Next is Olin, leaving only Otis safe in the nest with his parents. Can Odin and Ossana keep their babies fed and safe from predators until they are old enough to fly and hunt for themselves?

Made in the USA
Monee, IL
27 November 2023